THIS NOTEBOOK BELONGS TO

Made in the USA
Monee, IL
13 May 2022